KRAGOS
AND KILDOR
THE TWO-HEADED
DEMON

With special thanks to Cherith Baldry

For Ruby

www.beastquest.co.uk

ORCHARD BOOKS
338 Euston Road, London NW1 3BH
Orchard Books Australia
Level 17/207 Kent St, Sydney, NSW 2000

A Paperback Original
First published in Great Britain in 2009

Beast Quest is a registered trademark of Working Partners Limited
Series created by Working Partners Limited, London

Text © Working Partners Limited 2009
Cover and inside illustrations by Steve Sims © Orchard Books 2009

A CIP catalogue record for this book is available
from the British Library.

ISBN 978 1 40830 436 5

13

Printed and bound by CPI Group (UK) Ltd, Croydon, CR0 4YY

The paper and board used in this paperback are natural recyclable
products made from wood grown in sustainable forests. The
manufacturing processes conform to the environmental regulations of
the country of origin.

Orchard Books is a division of Hachette Children's Books,
an Hachette UK company.

www.hachette.co.uk

KRAGOS AND KILDOR THE TWO-HEADED DEMON

BY ADAM BLADE

ORCHARD BOOKS

THE ICY

THE

THE NORTHERN
MOUNTAINS

THE FOREST
OF FEAR

WESTERN OCEAN

TH

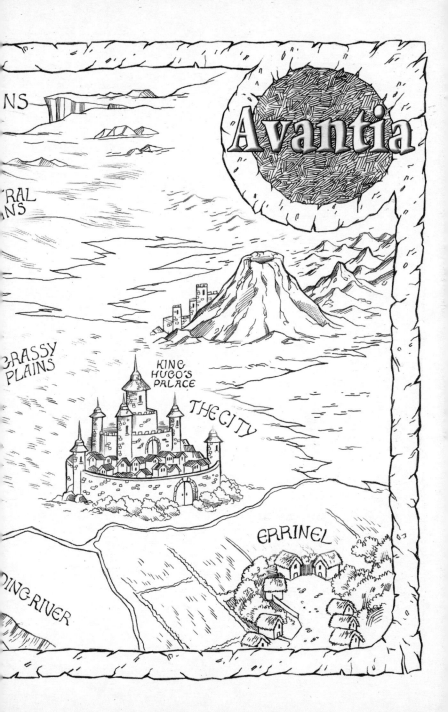

A FIERY SECRET

Dear Friend,

Thanks to my son, Tom, Avantia is now a place of peace. The kingdom is free of Wizard Malvel's dark magic and evil Beasts no longer roam its plains. Malvel has been banished to the darkness, a shadow of himself. Or so we like to believe...

All around me people are celebrating, but in my heart I know that something is not right. Disquiet twists and turns in my gut. I sense that Malvel is on the prowl once more. He schemes, he plots, and looks for a way to return to full strength, to tear Avantia apart.

I hope I am wrong. And if I am not, I hope that my brave son can stop him...

Taladon the Swift

CHAPTER ONE

A HERO'S RETURN

"Hold tight, Elenna!" Tom cried. His friend wrapped her arms tightly round Tom's waist.

He dug his heels into Storm's side; the black stallion thundered along the road. But however hard they tried, they couldn't catch the chestnut horse galloping ahead of them.

"You win!" Tom gasped, as the two horses, one after the other, flashed past a pine tree standing at a bend in the road.

He slowed Storm to a walk and glanced over his shoulder to see Elenna flushed with excitement. "They don't call your father Taladon the Swift for nothing!" she exclaimed with a broad grin.

"You ride well, Tom." Taladon's eyes shone with approval. He patted the glossy neck of his chestnut stallion. "There aren't many horses who could keep up with Fleetfoot."

Bright sunlight shone down on the green hills of Avantia. Tom's heart swelled with happiness as he urged Storm to a trot again, and gazed at the white road winding ahead.

"I can't wait to see Uncle Henry's

face when we get to Errinel," he said to his father. "He'll never expect to find you on his doorstep!"

Taladon smiled. "It's all thanks to you," he said.

Tom's father had been missing for many years, imprisoned in the dungeons of the evil sorcerer, Malvel. He had finally escaped when Tom weakened Malvel's magic by defeating him three times. But Taladon had been doomed to exist only as a ghost until Tom recovered the six pieces of the Amulet of Avantia. And in the struggle for the final piece, Tom had wounded Malvel, banishing him from the kingdom.

Tom could hardly believe that his father was riding with him now, fit and strong again, his face glowing with life.

Storm tossed his head, his bridle jingling as he let out a whinny of approval. Silver, Elenna's grey wolf, joined in with a joyful howl as he bounded along beside the horses.

Taladon rode in silence, but Tom saw a shadow of anxiety pass over his face. *What is he thinking?* Tom wondered. *Surely Malvel is too weak to do us any more harm?*

A moment later Taladon was smiling again. "I hope Maria has made some of her lamb stew," he said. "I haven't tasted it for years."

Tom shook off his fears. Maybe he had just imagined his father's worried look. "I'm sure she'll make it for you," he said. "And we'll be all together as a family at last!"

Tom's heart raced with excitement as he jumped down from Storm and knocked on the door of Uncle Henry's cottage. The sun was going down; smoke curled up from the chimney, and the sound of hammering came from his uncle's forge next door.

Tom exchanged a delighted grin with Elenna and his father as they waited on the doorstep. *All my Beast Quests were worth it, just for this!* he thought.

Footsteps approached the door and it was flung open. Aunt Maria stood in the doorway. "Taladon!" she exclaimed, her eyes wide with shock. "Is it really you?"

"It really is," Taladon replied with a smile. "It's good to see you again, Maria."

Aunt Maria stepped forward and drew Taladon into a hug. "What happened to you?" she asked. "Where have you been? Why didn't you *tell* us?"

Taladon drew back gently, smiling down at her. "It's a long story."

"Tom! Elenna!" Tears welled up in Aunt Maria's eyes. "You're safe! I never dared hope we'd be all together again."

"It's thanks to Tom." Taladon gave Tom a warm, affectionate look. "He's a real hero."

"I couldn't have done it without Elenna," Tom said, feeling himself turn red with embarrassment.

"I'm proud of you both," Aunt Maria said. "You'll want to see Henry," she added to Taladon. "He's in the forge."

"We'll go over there now," said Taladon. "Come on, Tom, Elenna."

"I'll stay and help settle Silver and the horses," Elenna said quickly. Tom guessed she wanted to give him and his father some time alone with Uncle Henry.

Tom led the way along the path from the cottage to the forge. As he pushed open the door, he felt a surge of heat from the fire that always burned there. The flames glowed with a fierce red light.

The sound of hammering stopped. Tom saw Uncle Henry standing in front of his anvil, a hammer in one hand and tongs holding a half-forged horseshoe in the other.

"There's someone here to see you," Tom said. He stepped inside and stood back to let his father follow.

Henry's mouth gaped wide and his eyes welled with tears. "Taladon!" he gasped.

"Hello, brother," Taladon said.

The hammer and the horseshoe

clanged on the stone floor of the
forge as Henry flung them aside and
ran to embrace his brother. "I can't
believe it!" he exclaimed. "I thought
you were dead."

"I was as good as dead." Taladon drew back from his brother and stood with his hands on Henry's shoulders. "But thanks to Tom, I'm as strong as ever. And now I'm home."

"It's wonderful to have you here. And you too, Tom." Uncle Henry gave Tom a hug. "Let's go and eat."

Back at the cottage, Tom and the others found his aunt and Elenna in the kitchen. Aunt Maria was stirring a large iron pot over the fire. Tom helped Elenna to set out pewter plates on the table.

Taladon sniffed the air. "Is that lamb stew I smell?"

Aunt Maria looked up from her cooking, a broad smile on her face. "I remembered it was your favourite! But you'll have to wait a while. I wasn't expecting guests."

She added some chopped onions to the pot. "We'll have to hold a feast in your honour, Taladon," she said.

"There's no need for that," Taladon protested.

"Nonsense!" Aunt Maria gave the pot another vigorous stir. "The whole of Errinel should know how much you have done for Avantia. What better excuse could we have for a feast? We'll invite the whole village."

The sun was going down. Elenna finished setting the table while Tom lit the lamps. When the meal was ready, everyone sat down in front of steaming bowls.

Tom glanced round the table at the faces of the people who meant so much to him. *I never dared to hope we would all be sitting together like this*, he thought. Raising his cup, he added aloud, "I can't remember the last time I felt this happy!"

A loud crash woke Tom. He sat bolt upright, for a moment unsure where he was. Then he recognised his old bedroom in the attic of his uncle and aunt's cottage. Pale dawn light was seeping through the shutters.

On the opposite side of the room, Elenna pushed back her blankets. "What was that?" she asked, her voice heavy with sleep.

"I don't know." Tom jumped up and dragged on his tunic. "We'd better go and find out."

Silver, who had been sleeping at the bottom of Elenna's bed, dashed out after them. Taladon joined them as they clattered down the stairs. In the passage below, Uncle Henry and Aunt Maria were already up; Henry was unbolting the outer door of the cottage.

Tom led the way as everyone poured outside. Nothing stirred as he glanced around.

Then his gaze fell on the forge. "Look at that!" he gasped.

The rays of the rising sun showed a huge, splintered hole in the door of the forge. It looked as if something had kicked its way inside.

Tom's stomach churned. *What made that hole?* he asked himself. *And is it still lurking inside the forge?*

CHAPTER TWO

A BEAST IN THE VILLAGE

Uncle Henry pounded down the path towards the forge, with Taladon and Aunt Maria just behind. Tom was about to follow when he noticed a golden flicker in the shadow of the trees beyond the forge.

He gripped Elenna's arm. "What's that?" he whispered.

"I don't know," she said, narrowing

her eyes. "But we can find out."

Side by side, Tom and Elenna skirted the walls of the forge and approached the edge of the forest until they could get a better view of what was lurking there. Silver padded beside Elenna, his fur bristling. Tom's heart started to thump as the creature came into view.

It had a man's body, tall and powerful, with two heads rising from between its shoulders. One of them was like a ram, with huge, curling horns, while the other was the head of an antlered stag. The upper part of the body had the dappled, velvety-brown coat of a deer; the creature's legs were covered in course, short, pale fur, and ended in pointed ram's hooves.

Around its waist it wore a thick leather belt, studded with razor-sharp

silver discs. Tiny golden flames licked
all around the fearsome creature, so
that it stood inside a shimmering
globe of golden light. Both heads
were turned towards the forge,
gazing fixedly at it; so far they hadn't
noticed Tom and Elenna.

"A Beast!" Elenna breathed.

Every detail burned into Tom's mind, recorded in the powerful memory he had gained when he defeated the evil sea monster, Narga. Fury rushed through him at the sight of the two-headed monster so close to his home.

From the stable behind the cottage Tom heard Storm let out an anxious whinny, as if he had sensed the evil presence lurking nearby.

Tom groped for the hilt of his sword, but in the rush to leave the cottage he hadn't buckled on his sword belt.

"I have to go back for my weapon," he said grimly – but before he could move his father sped past him, a hammer from the forge in his hand.

"Keep back!" Taladon ordered. "Guard the cottage!"

The huge Beast swung round and let out a roar as he spotted Tom's father. But instead of attacking him, the creature raced away into the forest, its stride lithe and fast. Taladon plunged after it among the trees. For a moment Tom could still see the golden light flickering through the branches; then it was gone.

"We've never seen that Beast before," he said to Elenna. "Do you think it's one of Malvel's servants?"

"I'm sure it is," she replied. "Maybe it was the Beast that kicked in the door of the forge?"

Tom snorted. "It must have been. I'm certain Malvel sent it – but what does it want here?" He paused, an icy sensation trickling down his spine. "Maybe it was meant to kill us all, in revenge for when I wounded Malvel."

"Then why did it break into the forge and not the cottage?" Elenna asked.

Before he could reply, Tom spotted movement at the edge of the trees. Taladon reappeared, striding rapidly back toward the forge. He passed Tom and Elenna, hardly seeming to notice them; Tom's heart lurched at the look of panic and fury in his father's eyes.

"No, no, no…" Taladon muttered as he marched past and vanished through the splintered door.

Tom exchanged a glance of alarm with Elenna and ran after his father, Silver bounding alongside. They met Uncle Henry at the doorway. Beyond him, Tom could see Taladon about to plunge his hand into the flames of the forge.

"No!" Tom yelled. He couldn't believe that his father would deliberately hurt himself. "Stop!"

Taladon's teeth were clenched and his eyes screwed shut, but he didn't hesitate as he thrust his hand into the fire.

Tom ran forwards, but Uncle Henry was already beside the fire, dragging

his brother away. For a moment
Taladon resisted, then gave in and
staggered back. His hand was seared
red from the heat, and his face was
white with pain.

"Are you mad?" Uncle Henry demanded. He grabbed Taladon's hand and plunged it into the tub of water next to the forge.

"What's going on?" Tom rushed to his father's side. "Why did you do that?"

"Taladon!" Aunt Maria gasped. She pulled off her apron and soaked it in the water tub. Then she wrung it out and brought it to Taladon.

Tom's father was breathing heavily. The skin on his burnt hand was beginning to peel away. He wrapped it in the wet apron that Aunt Maria handed to him. His voice was low and shaking with anger as he looked up at them. "The Cup of Life has been stolen!"

CHAPTER THREE

THE CUP
OF LIFE

"What's the Cup of Life?" Elenna
asked.

Tom gazed anxiously at his father.
Beads of sweat stood out on Taladon's
forehead and his teeth were clenched
with anger and pain. At last he let
out a long sigh.

"The Cup of Life is one of the
greatest magical treasures of Avantia,"

he explained. "Anyone who drinks from this golden goblet can repel death."

"And it was here, in my forge?" Uncle Henry's eyes were wide with astonishment.

"Many years ago," Taladon went on, "before Malvel imprisoned me, King Hugo gave me the cup to guard. I placed it here in the forge, because these flames are the hottest in Avantia, and they never go out. The cup has to be kept in fire at all times, or its magic won't work."

"Then that *was* one of Malvel's Beasts!" Tom exclaimed, fury welling up inside him. "Only Malvel would be evil enough to steal the Cup of Life."

Elenna nodded. "If he drinks from the cup he'll be strong again. And then he can launch another attack on Avantia."

"You're right," said Taladon. "It's vital that we get the cup back before Malvel has the chance to drink from it."

Tom spun round, ready to rush out of the forge, then he halted. "How can we do that?" he asked. "For all we know, Malvel is drinking from the cup right now."

Taladon shook his head. "Things aren't as bad as that. The cup loses its magic once it is taken out of the fire. It will need to be placed in blazing hot flames and left to rest there for at least a day before its power will work again. The cup glows golden when its magic is restored."

"So there is a chance!" Relief flooded over Tom. "Come on, Elenna. We'll leave right away."

"I'll come with you," his father said.

"You will not!" Aunt Maria stepped in Taladon's way before he could leave the forge. "You can't go chasing Beasts and battling wizards with your sword-hand burnt like that. It will take days to heal. I have a herbal ointment that will help, but it isn't magic. The healing will still take time."

"But I—" Taladon began.

"It's best if you stay here," Uncle Henry interrupted. "The Beast might come back, and if you all go, there'll be no one to protect the village."

Taladon gripped Tom's shoulder with his uninjured hand. "All right, Tom. I know you have the courage and strength to face this Beast."

Tom felt warm with pride at his father's praise. "We won't let you down," he promised. "Malvel will never drink from the Cup of Life!"

Elenna was standing beside the door of the forge. Her eyes were sparkling with excitement, while Silver's plumy tail waved and he sniffed the air, as if he couldn't wait to get on the trail of the Beast.

"Come on," Tom said. "Let's go and saddle Storm."

As he led the way towards the stable, Tom felt himself tingling with anticipation.

"I didn't expect our visit to end like this," Elenna admitted in a low voice.

Tom smiled. "I know what you mean. But we'll never turn away from a Beast Quest, will we?"

Elenna shook her head. "Never," she said.

It was all Tom needed to hear.

CHAPTER FOUR

ON THE TRAIL
OF THE BEAST

The sun was high in the sky by the
time Tom and Elenna set out. Aunt
Maria had insisted on feeding them
breakfast, and she had packed food
for their journey in Tom's saddlebags.

"Take care," Taladon said to Tom
as they parted. "The Cup of Life is
Malvel's last hope. He'll be desperate,
and that means he'll be more
dangerous than ever."

"You can trust us," Tom assured him.

"I know." Taladon smiled for the first time since the Cup of Life had vanished. "My son can defeat any Beast that ever lived."

Mounted on Storm, with Elenna riding behind him, Tom headed for the trees where he had spotted the Beast. Silver padded beside the black stallion, his nose to the ground.

"That's right, boy!" Elenna said encouragingly. "Sniff out the Beast for us!"

Tom guided Storm into the forest, looking out for the flicker of gold that might show him that the Beast was close by. *But he'll be long gone by now*, he thought. *We'll have to hope that we can catch up with him.*

They were still on the outskirts of the forest when Tom heard a rustle

46

in the undergrowth.

Elenna's grip tightened round his waist. "What's that?"

Tensing, Tom began to draw his sword. Then he relaxed as a young animal stepped into the open, looking up at him with huge, trusting eyes. "It's only a deer," he exclaimed.

"That's a really frightening Beast!"
Elenna laughed. "No, Silver!" she
added a moment later, as the great
wolf lowered his head and let out a
throaty growl. "He's not dangerous."

But Silver's growl deepened; Elenna
slid down from Storm's back and
stroked her pet until he gradually
calmed down.

"I don't know what's the matter with him," she said to Tom.

Tom shrugged. "Maybe he's just nervous." A tiny prickle of doubt disturbed him; Silver's instincts had always been right so far. But Tom pushed his doubts down. What harm could a deer do? "Let's get on," he said.

He turned Storm along a path that wound through the trees, deeper into the forest. Elenna walked beside the horse, her hand resting on Silver's thick fur. The little deer followed a few paces behind.

The trees grew thicker; the branches criss-crossed overhead, almost cutting off the light of the sun. Tom still couldn't see any sign of the Beast, but he noticed that all the birds were quiet, as if something terrifying had passed by not long before.

"Look there!" Elenna exclaimed at last. She halted, pointing at something beside the path.

Tom dismounted, and made out the marks of huge cloven hoofs, sunk deep into the mossy ground. "Those are the prints of the Beast!" he exclaimed, remembering the creature's shaggy ram's legs.

Leading Storm through the thick undergrowth, Tom followed the tracks. Silver kept his nose close to the ground, pressing forward eagerly, with Elenna walking quietly at his side. The deer stayed with them, though it kept well away from the tracks, picking its way along the edge of the path.

"I think the deer is scared of these tracks," Elenna said.

As the trail led them deeper into the heart of the forest, Tom noticed that the trees ahead of him were outlined by a strange light. It was pale and silver, not the golden glow that had surrounded the Beast. Nevertheless, Tom drew his sword, and signalled to Elenna to be quiet. *I'm not taking any chances*, he thought. *That could be Malvel!*

Tom peered round the trunk of a giant oak tree into a clearing beyond. Outlined in a shimmering silver globe was the image of a man. He had a wispy white beard and wore a robe embroidered with magical signs.

"Aduro!" Tom exclaimed, rushing toward the vision.

Anxiety surged over him as he drew to a halt before the good wizard. Aduro's face was pinched and drawn, and Tom could see the outlines of trees through his form, as if Aduro didn't have the strength to hold the image steady.

"What's the matter?" he asked. "Why are you—?"

Aduro held up a hand to silence him. "I haven't much time," he began. His voice was weak and shaky. "My strength is fading fast.

Listen carefully, Tom. I know all about your Quest to find the Cup of Life."

Tom exchanged an amazed glance with Elenna. She was standing beside him, with Storm and Silver; Tom caught a glimpse of the deer slipping behind her into the shadows, as if it was afraid of the wizard.

"We're tracking the Beast that took the cup," Elenna explained. "It's huge, with two heads – one like a ram and the other like a stag."

Aduro nodded. "I know this Beast." His voice was so feeble that Tom could hardly hear him. "There is more to your Quest than meets the eye. It's vital to recover the cup so Malvel can't drink from it and be revived. But that's not all. The future of Avantia and its leaders depends on your Quest."

Cold horror began to creep through Tom. "What do you mean?"

"If the Cup of Life isn't found by the next full moon, the fire at the heart of Avantia's leaders will go out forever." Wizard Aduro's voice shook. "King Hugo and I will become half-people, stranded somewhere between life and death. Worse – we will turn our backs on the kingdom we love."

"But that – that would mean Malvel could take over Avantia!" Tom protested.

"True," Aduro said hoarsely. "And there would be nothing the King or I could do to stop him. Already our strength is failing."

Elenna let out a gasp of dismay. "The next full moon – that's only three nights away!"

"Then we have three nights," Tom said. Realising how important his Quest was, he straightened up, gripping his sword determinedly. "We'll find the Beast that stole the cup and get it back."

Aduro nodded. "I expect no less of you, Tom, and you, Elenna. The Beast is close by, and I came to give you the knowledge you need to conquer him. His name is Kragos and Kildor."

"Two names!" Elenna exclaimed.

"That is because this Beast has two natures." Summoning all his strength, Aduro muttered a few words under his breath. A grimace of pain crossed his face as he flung out his hands in a wide gesture.

Tom took a step back as an image formed in the air between him and the wizard. It was a Beast with two heads: one a grey, snarling wolf, the other a fox with bright, cunning eyes.

Almost immediately the form of the Beast flickered and bent, and a new image appeared; this time it looked like the Beast Tom and Elenna had seen fleeing into the forest, with a stag's head and a ram's head. Then Wizard Aduro sagged, exhausted, and the vision vanished.

"Why did you show us two different Beasts?" Tom asked.

"It is the same Beast," Wizard Aduro explained, his breath coming in shallow gasps. "Kragos and Kildor regenerate their form with every generation. But one thing remains constant: he always has two natures." He paused and then went on. "In a way, he is like the contradictions of life. Day is always followed by night. Good is always challenged by evil. But remember this, Tom: Kragos and

Kildor will always use his double nature to attack."

Aduro's voice began to fade. The silver globe where he was standing flickered and went out, and the image of the wizard vanished with it. Tom and Elenna were left standing in the darkening forest.

Tom turned to his friend, struggling to shake off the full horror of what he had just seen.

"I don't care how evil this Beast is," he declared. "I'll defeat him and get the cup back, if it's the last thing I do!"

CHAPTER FIVE

DANGER IN THE JUNGLE

Tom and the others pressed on through the forest, still following the tracks of Kragos and Kildor's cloven hooves. The little deer had emerged from the undergrowth when Wizard Aduro disappeared, and trotted along trustingly beside Tom.

"I think we've got a new animal friend!" Elenna laughed. "Maybe he saw the Beast, and thinks we'll be able to protect him."

Silver let out a long howl, gazing threateningly at the deer but keeping well away. Storm flung up his head, his bridle jingling as if something had spooked him.

"I think Silver's jealous," Elenna said, patting her wolf friend's back.

"Storm, too," Tom grinned at her. "But it looks as if they'll have to get used to him."

Gradually Tom noticed that the forest around them was changing. The ground underfoot was softer, covered with a layer of debris. The air had turned warmer, with a tang of rotting vegetation. The trees grew even closer to each other, and thick vines hung from the branches.

Tom drew Storm to an abrupt halt

as a snake slithered across the track
and vanished into a hollow tree
trunk. "I know where we are!" he
exclaimed. "This is the Dark Jungle,
where we fought Claw the Giant
Monkey."

Elenna shuddered as she glanced round. "I remember. It's just the sort of place where Kragos and Kildor might be lurking."

The daylight was dying; soon silver moonbeams pierced the tangle of branches overhead. "The moon's nearly full," Tom said. He struggled to control his anxiety as he looked up and caught a glimpse of it floating above the trees. He suppressed a weary sigh. "We only have two more nights after this."

"We need to make camp," Elenna pointed out. "We can't keep going all day and all night."

"But then we'll risk losing the Beast," Tom argued.

"You won't defeat the Beast if you're exhausted," Elenna retorted. "You need to rest."

"Maybe you're right," Tom sighed reluctantly.

As soon as they came to a clearing where the clammy air of the jungle felt fresher, he unsaddled Storm and left him to graze, while Silver hunted. Elenna took out some of the food from the saddlebags. "There's fruit over there," she said, pointing to a nearby tree. "I'm going to pick some. We need to make our provisions last as long as we can."

"Do you think we should feed the deer?" Tom suggested. Glancing round, he noticed that the creature had vanished. "What happened to our new friend?" he asked.

"I don't know. I didn't see him go," Elenna replied. "Maybe he—"

She broke off as a squeal of fear came from the darkness under the

trees. Tom spun round, drawing
his sword.

"That sounds like him!" he
exclaimed. "Something must have
caught him."

The terrified squeal came again. Tom
rushed across the clearing towards the
sound, with Elenna close behind.

When Tom reached the edge of the
clearing he was confronted by a wall
of green leaves and stalks, with thick
vines twining through them. Hacking
at them with his sword, he forced his

way forward. His muscles ached with the effort, but he kept going. The squeals grew more panic-stricken, spurring him on.

Tom glanced round to see Elenna as she unslung her bow from her shoulder and fitted an arrow to the string. He was glad to have her close behind him, keeping watch for anything that might attack.

At last the vines began to thin out. Only a few thick stems blocked Tom's way. Beyond them, he could see the deer; vines trailed around his legs as if they were trapping him.

But the deer wasn't struggling. It was motionless, watching Tom and Elenna expectantly. Its eyes narrowed. Tom thought the glint he saw there looked almost cruel. Then he shook off the thought. *The light is so bad here, I'm starting to see things! He's frightened, that's all.*

Bracing himself, Tom swung his sword back and struck at the thick vine in front of him, slicing it in two. The cut ends whipped back at him; instinctively Tom used the flat of his sword to bat them away. But instead of falling, the cut ends hovered menacingly over him.

"Oh no...it's alive!" Tom let out a cry of alarm as the jungle around him suddenly seethed with movement. The vines in the nearby trees lunged towards him.

"Tom!" Elenna yelled. "Watch out!"

Tom stepped back, but it was too late. A thick vine wrapped around his calf. He raised his sword to cut through it, but another vine twisted around his arm. A third vine coiled round his waist; he was knocked off his feet, the breath driven from his body as he landed on his back.

Beyond the thrashing vines Tom looked up, straight into the face of the deer. This time there was no mistake. The little creature's eyes glowed with triumph. *He led me here deliberately!* Tom thought, as he struggled to free himself. *But why?*

The vines dragged Tom into the tangled undergrowth. No matter how much he struggled, he couldn't stop himself from being dragged along, tree roots tearing at his back. Behind him, Elenna's bowstring twanged again and again. Her arrows bit deep into the tendrils that held Tom captive, but their grip didn't relax.

Trying to sit up, Tom struck out with his sword. Thank goodness he still had it. But a thick stem lashed down at his arm and knocked the weapon out of his hand.

"No!" Tom let out a roar of frustration.

He twisted round. To his relief he saw Elenna grab his sword and chase after him as the vines dragged him further into the undergrowth.

"Don't give up, Tom!" she called. "I'm coming!"

Suddenly the undergrowth parted. Just ahead, lit up by a shaft of moonlight, Tom saw a huge green pod, as tall as a man. As the vines carried him closer, leaves peeled away from its sides, leaving a dark opening at the top. Tom let out a yell as the vines lifted him off his feet. They swung him into the air, and dropped him through the hole into the pod.

He landed feet first, splashing waist-deep into sticky liquid. As it soaked through his clothes he felt his skin start to burn. At the same moment, the leaves closed over the opening, leaving him trapped.

Forcing down panic, Tom pushed at the wall of the pod, but it felt like tough leather, impossible to break through. He tugged out his belt knife and stabbed at it, but the small blade slid uselessly off the surface.

In the dim, greenish light Tom saw razor-sharp teeth suddenly slide out of the wall. Startled, he stepped back, only to feel more teeth pricking him from behind.

"Elenna! Help!" he shouted, his voice muffled by the pod.

He heard a faint sucking noise. The burning liquid gradually began to creep up his chest. Tom realised the pod walls were closing in. Already he could feel the countless teeth fastening themselves onto his body.

What am I going to do? he asked himself. *This plant is eating me alive!*

CHAPTER SIX

FACE TO FACE

Tom struggled to climb up to the top of the pod, but the walls were smooth; there was nothing he could hold on to except for the sharp spines that were slowly sinking into his flesh.

"Elenna, help!" he called again.

Suddenly a bright sword blade stabbed through the wall of the pod, barely missing Tom's face and slicing off a lock of his hair.

"I'm here, Tom!" Elenna called out, her voice ringing clearly through the gash.

The blade slashed downwards, tearing a ragged hole. The burning liquid began to drain away. As the sword hacked at the pod wall again, daylight poured through the gap, and Tom could see Elenna swinging his sword to cut him out.

Tearing himself free of the spines, Tom clambered out of the plant. During his struggle the moon had set, and the sky above the trees was growing brighter as morning approached.

Tom staggered with relief as he took in huge gulps of the cool dawn air. All around him the vines were twisting and flopping about on the ground. Gradually they grew still as the remains of the pod crumpled and died.

"Thanks!" Tom gasped, as he took his sword from Elenna. "I thought I was finished in there!"

"I was scared I was going to kill you with your own sword," his friend admitted. "But I had to do something."

Tom tore up a handful of grass to clean the sticky remains of the pod from his sword blade, then tried to wipe his soaked clothes. "I think we were lured into a trap," he said.

Elenna nodded. "I saw how the deer looked when the vines grabbed you." She bent down and started to pick up the arrows she had fired, glancing round nervously. "He seemed...happy!"

"I don't understand," Tom went on, frowning as he sheathed his sword and retrieved his belt knife from the wreckage of the pod. "The deer looked so harmless. I can't imagine why it would have wanted to trap us."

Elenna straightened up, suddenly turning pale, her eyes wide with fear. "We've left Storm and Silver without protection," she exclaimed.

"No!" Tom's heart pounded as he raced back towards the clearing with Elenna beside him.

To his relief, Storm was still cropping the grass at the edge of the clearing, while Silver sat nearby, his ears pricked alertly; he sprang to his feet as he saw Elenna.

"They're all right," she cried, rushing over to him.

The undergrowth suddenly rustled and the deer leapt into the open. The face that had looked so gentle was twisted with fury, and its large, innocent eyes were full of anger.

As Tom spun round to face it, his sword at the ready, the deer began to swell. Its legs grew longer and thicker, its body filled out, and huge antlers sprouted from its head. It had transformed into a mighty stag.

The stag let out a bellow. Rearing

on its hind legs, it slashed with its razor-sharp antlers at the foliage on the boughs above it.

Tom drew his sword again, gripping the hilt firmly. *Well, I can show my strength too!* he thought.

"That's Kragos!" Elenna exclaimed, dashing up to Tom's side. "He looks just like the stag part of the Beast that we saw outside the village."

"Now I understand!" Tom breathed. "The little deer must have been Kragos in disguise."

Elenna's eyes blazed with anger. "He pretended to be gentle, to lure us to that man-eating plant!"

Tom remembered Wizard Aduro's advice that this Beast would always attack in two ways. "Kragos and Kildor have managed to split themselves down the middle," he said. "The tracks we've been following must belong to Kildor, the ram part. And he still has the Cup of Life!"

Kragos was foaming at the mouth, his sharp hooves pawing at the ground, ready to charge. Tom narrowed his eyes, calling on the special battle skills he had gained from the amber jewel when he defeated Tusk the mighty mammoth.

"Take Storm and Silver somewhere safe," he told Elenna, never taking his eyes from the furious Beast.

He heard Elenna's footsteps retreating and a protesting howl from Silver as he was dragged away.

Tom took a step forward, bringing up his shield to cover his body and raising his sword. "Come on," he challenged the stag. "I'm ready for you!"

CHAPTER SEVEN

KRAGOS'S ESCAPE

The Beast let out another fearsome bellow. As he lowered his head to charge, the rays of the rising sun pierced the jungle canopy and glistened on his cruel antlers. He pawed the ground once more, and hurtled across the clearing.

Tom felt the ground shudder as Kragos charged towards him.

Planting his feet firmly, he braced himself for the impact.

The Beast smashed into Tom's shield. Tom staggered back from the force of the blow. Then, in one fluid movement, he lowered his shield and brought his sword up, swinging the blade out at the stag's muscular flank. He felt it bite deep into his enemy's flesh.

Kragos wheeled away, blood streaming down his leg. As he turned to face Tom, his eyes glared with anger, but Tom thought he could see wariness there, too.

Now he knows I can hurt him, he realised.

Tom raised his sword, ready to leap towards the Beast and finish him off. But before he could move, the sound of hunting horns rang out, and a party of huntsmen came crashing out of the undergrowth. They wore leather jerkins beneath green cloaks that billowed out behind them.

A flurry of arrows zipped through the air. Tom flung himself to the ground. But the arrows were not aimed at him. He lay flat as the huntsmen's horses thundered past him, in pursuit of Kragos – who they were hunting like an ordinary stag.

"No!" he yelled. "I almost had him!"
Tom raised his head to see Kragos
flee the clearing; he trampled a path
through the forest in the direction
Kildor's tracks were leading.

The hunters let off another volley of arrows and followed, smashing down bushes and saplings as they charged.

Tom picked himself up and grabbed his sword and shield. As the noise of the huntsmen died away, Elenna emerged from the trees at the opposite side of the clearing. She had re-saddled Storm and was leading him by his bridle, while Silver padded beside her.

Tom strode across the clearing to meet her. "I can't believe our bad luck!" he exclaimed, anger welling up inside him. "Kragos was weakening. If those hunters hadn't turned up just then, I could have beaten him!"

Elenna didn't reply. Her face was pale, and Tom noticed that her sleeve was torn and blood was trickling down her arm. "You're hurt!" he exclaimed.

"One of the hunters' arrows grazed my arm," Elenna told him. "But it's just a scratch. Don't worry about it." Her gaze travelled to the gap in the undergrowth where Kragos had vanished. "Stupid hunters!" she added furiously. "Couldn't they see it wasn't a normal stag?"

Tom shrugged, trying to suppress his own anger. "We'd better get moving," he said. "But I'll heal your arm first, with Epos's talon."

He wiped his sword blade and fitted it back into his sheath, then took the talon of Epos the flame bird from its slot on his shield. As he held it, he felt the many small wounds he had received from the sharp teeth of the pod suddenly close and heal. Fresh strength flooded through him.

Taking Elenna's arm, Tom laid the flame bird's talon against the scratch made by the arrow. The talon glowed, but the wound stayed the same.

"What's the matter?" Elenna asked. "Why isn't it working?"

"I don't know. It healed me just now…" Tom kept the talon pressed against Elenna's wound for a moment more, but the scratch still didn't heal. The arrow had bitten deep; blood was still oozing out of the wound and all around it Elenna's skin was reddened.

Tom felt a prickle of uneasiness as he returned Epos's talon to his shield and searched in his saddlebags for a bandage. "I wish we had some of Aunt Maria's healing herbs to make a poultice," he said as he wound the linen strip round Elenna's arm.

"I'll be fine," Elenna assured him. "With any luck, it won't be long before we're back in Errinel, and Aunt Maria can look at the wound then."

"Let's hope so," Tom replied.

Holding Storm's reins, he led the way across the clearing to where Kragos and the hunters had disappeared. The horses had churned up the earth so that Kildor's tracks had been destroyed. Silver padded up and down, sniffing and letting out a confused whine.

Tom kicked the ground. "We'll never be able to find Kildor now."

"We could follow these tracks," Elenna suggested uncertainly.

Tom shook his head. "Kragos would never lead the hunters to Kildor. There's no way to track him, or to find the cup."

As he was speaking a dim light appeared at the edge of the trees. Tom could just make out the figures of Wizard Aduro and King Hugo. They both looked tired and haggard, their eyes dead, staring at nothing.

Fear surged up inside Tom. "King Hugo! Aduro!" he exclaimed. "What is the matter?"

Neither of the men answered him. They didn't even seem to hear him.

"Why won't they talk to you?" Elenna asked, her voice full of anxiety.

"We still have two nights before the fire in their hearts goes out forever."

Tom hesitated. "I think Wizard Aduro must be sending us a vision of the future," he said at last. "This is what he and King Hugo *will* be like, if we fail in our Quest."

Elenna shuddered, turning her head away.

"Aduro must mean this as a message," Tom went on. "He's trying to tell us that we mustn't give up."

For a moment he felt swamped by the task ahead. Time was running out for his beloved kingdom, and he had lost the only trail that might lead him to the cup.

Tom clenched his fists. "I *won't* give up," he vowed, hoping that King Hugo and Wizard Aduro could hear him. "While there's blood in my veins, I'll go on looking for the Cup of Life. I'll never turn aside from my Quest!"

The vision began to fade. Tom fished in his pocket and brought out his father's compass, holding it up before him. The needle swung round to *Destiny*.

"Look!" Tom said to Elenna, pointing. "That's the way we have to go. To the Ruby Desert!"

DESTINY IN THE DESERT

Dear Friend,

As I feared, Malvel is searching for a way back to Avantia. He has sent his two-headed demon, Kragos and Kildor, to do his bidding – bringing with them double the evil. Now that they have the Cup of Life, the future of Avantia hangs in the balance. I know that somewhere the cup sits in a new fiery home. Malvel's Beast stands guard over the precious goblet. When it glows golden again, Malvel will drink from it and all will be lost.

My son and his brave friend, Elenna, face their biggest enemy yet – a Beast with twice the power and twice the evil. Can they find the Cup of Life and retrieve it? Or is Avantia doomed? It is almost too much for a father to contemplate. But I must watch Tom's progress, as best I can. And so must you...

Taladon the Swift

CHAPTER ONE

SEARCHING FOR WATER

On the edge of the desert, the heat was intense. Sweat plastered Tom's hair to his forehead and made his tunic cling to him. He had already journeyed once into the desert when he battled Vipero the snake man, and he didn't want to venture there again. But the needle of his father's compass had pointed this way, leading Tom and Elenna to the double-Beast Kragos and Kildor, and the stolen Cup of Life.

Elenna was mounted on Storm behind Tom. Tom heard her sigh as she leant against him. He glanced over his shoulder and saw that her face was pale.

"Are you all right?" he asked.

"I feel faint," Elenna admitted. "It must be the heat."

Worried, Tom gazed out across the rolling sand dunes. He didn't want to take Elenna into the desert if she was feeling ill. He fished out Taladon's compass from his pocket, hoping it might lead them in a different direction. But the needle swung between *Destiny* and *Danger*.

Then the Cup of Life must be somewhere in the desert, Tom told himself. *And danger is waiting for us there as well.*

Aloud he said, "We'd better find some water."

"There won't be any in the desert," Elenna pointed out. "Why don't we go to that town we visited before, on our Quest against Vipero? It's not far, and there's a well."

"Good idea," said Tom.

He turned Storm in the direction of the town. Thanks to the perfect memory given to him by the jewel he had won from Narga the sea monster, he had no need of a map to find the way.

Before long the dry grassland that bordered the desert gave way to rocks. The road climbed for a little way, then plunged into a deep ravine with sheer rock walls on either side. Storm's hooves rang on the stony path as he trotted between the cliffs. Tom heaved a huge sigh of relief to be sheltered from the harsh rays of the sun.

He blinked as his eyes became used to the shadow. When he could see clearly again, he looked up at the top of the cliffs. The sheer rock wall was crowned with huge boulders, outlined against the sky. They stretched along the entire length of the passage through the ravine.

"Do you think we should turn back and take a longer way round?" he asked Elenna.

"I don't know." His friend's voice was weary. "We really need water now."

Silver let out a whine of agreement.

"You're right," Tom said, dismissing his worries. "We haven't much time left to find the Cup of Life, and we can't head into the desert without water."

"Then let's get through the ravine as quickly as we can," Elenna suggested.

Tom nodded. "I know you're tired, boy," he said to Storm, patting the black stallion's sweat-soaked neck. "But just one good gallop, and you can have a rest, and all the water you want."

Storm flung up his head and gave a loud whinny. The thunder of his hooves echoed around the ravine as he hurtled forward. Elenna clung more tightly to Tom's waist, and Silver bounded alongside.

"Go, boy!" Tom shouted.

The end of the ravine, where the path plunged back into bright sunlight, was getting closer and closer.

Not far now, Tom thought, gripping Storm with his knees and bending low over his neck. *Not far, and then we'll be safe…*

Storm pounded along the rocky track at the bottom of the ravine. Sparks flew up from his hooves. The end of the ravine drew closer and closer.

Then Tom heard a threatening rumble, like distant thunder.

CHAPTER TWO

THE VALLEY OF ETERNAL FLAME

A huge section of the cliff face had torn free. Great swathes of rock were sliding down into the cleft, carrying earth and trees with them.

"No!" Tom yelled.

He knew there was no time to outrun the landslide. Tugging at Storm's reins with all his strength, he managed to turn the stallion back the way they had come. With an echoing boom, a massive rock slammed into the ground just behind them, throwing up a shower of rock chips and pebbles. Tom felt them sting and scratch his neck and shoulders. A whole tree crashed down and lodged itself across the ravine. It brought with it an avalanche of earth. Silver was closest to it; the wolf was knocked off his paws, legs flailing wildly as the earth engulfed him.

"Silver!" Elenna shouted, as Storm carried them past the place where her friend had disappeared. "Tom, stop!"

Tom glanced over his shoulder. He didn't want to leave Silver, but if they went back they would be caught in the roaring cascade of rocks and earth.

Then he saw Silver's muzzle and forepaws appear from a mound of soil. The grey wolf scrambled free and launched himself after Storm. Together they raced back along the ravine, while the thunder of the landslide died away behind them.

At last Tom drew Storm to a halt and looked back. Dust billowed into the air, stinging his eyes; he could taste grit in his mouth. A few smaller rocks still bounced down the cliff face, but the worst of the landslide was over. The road they had meant to take was completely blocked by rocks, earth and uprooted trees.

"Now what do we do?" Elenna asked, swiping her sleeve over her forehead. "We'll never reach the town this way."

For a moment Tom thought they would have to go the long way round. Then he remembered the purple jewel he had won in Gorgonia when he defeated Sting the scorpion man.

"What about this?" he asked, pulling the gem out of the slot on his belt. "It helps me cut through rock."

Elenna peered over his shoulder at the jewel, which shone with a murky purple light. "We could try," she said doubtfully. "How does it work?"

"I'm not sure," Tom replied. "I've

only used it once before, when we battled Sting."

He slid down from Storm and strode back along the ravine until he reached the blockage. Holding up the jewel so that the purple light shone down on the rocks, he commanded, "Split open!"

Nothing happened. The ravine was still blocked. All Tom could hear was the sound of hooves on rock as Elenna joined him, riding Storm. Silver padded beside them and let out a growl as he approached the rock-pile, shaking the loose earth out of his fur.

"Maybe you should cut the rock with your sword while you hold the jewel," Elenna suggested.

"I could try, but I don't want to ruin the blade," Tom said. He knew he would need his sword when he had to face the Beast.

Frustrated, he gripped the jewel tighter, and felt a faint tingling in his hand. "Maybe…" he began thoughtfully, and touched the jewel to the nearest boulder. "Maybe the jewel itself does the cutting…"

Purple light flashed out of the jewel, dancing on the surface of the rock. There was a hissing sound, followed by a creak that grew so loud Elenna winced and covered her ears with her hands.

Tom stared as the huge boulder split apart and began to crumble. A narrow passage opened up through the rocks and heaps of earth, until it was blocked again by the trunk of a fallen tree.

"It works!" Elenna grinned widely.

Cautiously, Tom walked forward.
When he reached the tree he
touched the jewel to the trunk. Light
shone out of it again, and the tree
trunk parted and shrivelled away
with a smell of burning.

"Come on!" he called to Elenna.

"We'll soon be through."

Storm tossed his head, reluctant to enter the narrow track, but Elenna coaxed him gently forward. Silver slunk along behind, his fur bristling as he sniffed at the crumbled rocks and scraps of tree bark.

With the power of the jewel, it wasn't long before Tom had forged a path through the rest of the earth and boulders that blocked the ravine. He heaved a sigh of relief as they reached the open ground beyond.

"Let's hurry," he said, tucking the purple jewel back into his belt and swinging himself into Storm's saddle, in front of Elenna. "We don't want to risk another avalanche."

Once again Tom urged his tired horse into a gallop. Soon they left

the ravine behind and came out
onto a rocky slope that ended in a
stretch of thin, dusty grassland.

"There's the town," Elenna said,
pointing to where the sand-coloured
walls rose out of the plain.

Tom could tell she was trying to be
cheerful, but she was leaning against
him heavily and he could feel the
burning heat of her body through
his tunic. Glancing back he saw that
her face was paler than ever and her
eyes were glazed with fever.

"You don't look well," he said
worriedly. "Are you sure you should—"

"I'm fine," Elenna interrupted. "Or
I will be, once I've had some water."

The sun was blazing down by the
time they reached the town. The
doors and window shutters were
closed on the houses they passed,

and they saw hardly anyone about in the streets.

"Anyone with any sense rests at this time of day," Elenna said hoarsely.

The town's main square was empty when Tom and Elenna reached it, except for a couple of dogs sprawled in the shade of a deserted market stall.

Tom guided Storm over to the well and slid down from his back. Elenna swayed as she tried to dismount. Tom grabbed her and helped her to the ground. She slumped onto the paving stones, sitting with her back against the well, her head in her hands. Silver pushed his muzzle against her shoulder with a questioning whine.

Tom gazed at his friend, his anxiety growing. He'd seen Elenna tired and thirsty before, but never like this. Quickly he unwound the chain and

let the bucket down into the well.
When he pulled it up again it was
brimming with cool water.

Several earthenware beakers were
standing on top of the well for
travellers to drink from. Tom filled
one from the bucket and handed it
to Elenna; she drained it in one long
gulp, and held it out for more. When
Tom had refilled it, and taken
another for himself, he set down the
bucket so that their animal friends
could drink.

"This is thirsty weather for travelling," a voice behind him said.

Tom spun round. A desert nomad stood near the well; Tom hadn't heard him approach. Bright eyes in a lined, sunburnt face looked out from under the hood of a sand-coloured robe. He was leading a grey horse, with a laden pack mule following just behind.

"Yes…yes, it is," Tom stammered. "Have you come far?"

"Out of the desert." The nomad gestured in the direction of the distant sand dunes. "I've come to trade for supplies for my people."

Tom was surprised that anyone could live out in the desert, and wondered what they could possibly have to trade.

"We travelled in the desert once," Elenna said. Her voice was weak, but to Tom's relief she was looking more alert.

"Then you were lucky to come out alive," the nomad told her. "The Ruby Desert has no pity for strangers."

As the animals had finished drinking, Tom let the bucket down into the well again. When he had pulled it up, he refilled their water bottles, then offered the rest of the water to the nomad.

"What's the hottest place in the desert?" Tom asked, remembering how the Cup of Life had to be placed in fire before its magic would work.

The nomad dipped his beaker and took a drink. "That would be the Valley of Eternal Flame," he replied, his bright eyes fixed on Tom. "The fire there never goes out."

Tom exchanged an excited glance with Elenna. *That's the place we should make for*, he thought. "Where is it?" he asked the nomad.

The man pointed towards the sand dunes. "But you should not even think of seeking it out," he warned Tom. "The heat is so great that the cacti around it burst into flame. Even my people don't go there."

Elenna was already scrambling to her feet. Tom climbed into Storm's saddle and pulled her up after him. Silver let out a long howl, his tail waving eagerly.

"Thank you," Tom said to the nomad. "You've been a big help."

He urged Storm into a canter, heading for the edge of town.

"Young fools!" the nomad shouted after them.

But Tom paid him no attention. Excitement surged through him. *Now we know where to find Kragos and Kildor*, he thought. *We'll soon get back the Cup of Life!*

CHAPTER THREE

FIRE IN THE DESERT

The sun beat down on Tom and Elenna as they struck out into the desert. Sand dunes rose all around them, bare except for a few clumps of cacti, and here and there a shrivelled bush. The air was hot and dry; Tom's mouth felt parched, but he knew they had to save their precious water for as long as they could.

Storm's hooves sounded muffled on the sand. Sometimes he would sink in as the soft surface gave way, and struggle to regain his footing. Silver padded along in the shade alongside the stallion; Tom could hear him panting.

At first Elenna had seemed stronger, buoyed up by the excitement of drawing closer to the end of their Quest. But the heat soon drained her strength. She sagged against Tom again. When he glanced back he saw that she was resting her head on his shoulder, her eyes closed.

"Elenna?" he said, worried that she would lose her grip on his waist and fall off. "Wake up!"

Elenna's eyes flickered open and she peered blearily at Tom. "Are we there?" she asked.

"Not yet. Elenna, you can't go on like this."

"Yes, I can." Elenna sounded as stubborn as ever. "I'm just thirsty. And my arm feels worse."

"What?" said Tom in alarm. "You didn't tell me. Let me have a look at it."

He slid from Storm and helped Elenna down beside him. She crumpled to the ground as if her legs wouldn't hold her up. The bandage still covered the wound made by the hunter's arrow. Her arm looked red and puffy.

Tom unfastened the bandage. The gash had stopped bleeding, but had turned a deep purple colour. Streaks of red stretched from it all along Elenna's arm.

Cold fear settled in Tom's stomach.

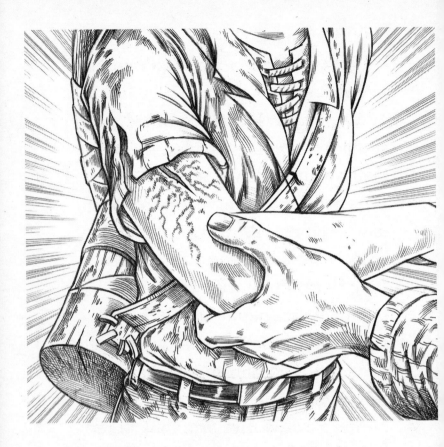

"I think the arrow must have been poisoned," he said.

"Maybe it was. But I'm fine, Tom, really." Elenna said determinedly. "The wound can wait till we get back to Errinel, and then your Aunt Maria will know what to do."

That might be too late, Tom thought.

Bending over Elenna's arm, he sucked at the wound in an effort to draw out the poison. Elenna let out a small whimper of pain. As he spat into the sand, Tom realised that he wasn't doing her any good. *If I'd thought of this to begin with, it might have helped*, he scolded himself. *But the poison is deep inside her now.*

"I'm strong, Tom. I can fight it off," Elenna assured him.

Tom nodded, struggling to keep back tears of desperation. However brave his friend was, he knew she couldn't last much longer, especially in the fierce heat of the Ruby Desert.

What was he going to do?

Suddenly he heard an excited yelp from Silver. Looking round, Tom saw the wolf digging vigorously at the roots of a straggling bush with grey-green leaves.

"What have you got there, boy?" he asked.

Sand sprayed up behind Silver as his scrabbling paws dug deeper still.

"He's found something," Elenna said.

Suddenly Tom recognised the bush. "That's sagebrush!" he exclaimed. "Aunt Maria uses the root to treat scrapes and scratches. Silver, you're brilliant!"

Tom dashed over to the bush and helped the grey wolf to dig, scooping the sand out of the hole with both hands, then using the edge of his shield to dig deeper. Even Storm trotted over and scraped at the sand with one fore-hoof.

At last the sand was cleared away from the fleshy roots of the sagebrush. Tom took out his belt knife and cut one of them off. Taking it back to Elenna, he split the root in half and squeezed out the juices onto his friend's wound.

Her arm didn't look any different, but Elenna let out a long sigh. "That feels so much better! Thank you, Tom."

"Thank Silver!"

The grey wolf came nosing up to Elenna. She flung her arms around him and gave him a big hug. "You're so clever!" she praised him.

Tom went back to the hole and cut off more of the healing root. Stowing it in his saddlebag, he mounted Storm and helped Elenna up.

"Let's go!" he said. "The Valley of Eternal Flame can't be far now!"

The air grew hotter still as Tom and Elenna ventured further into the desert. At last Tom spotted a dot of light glowing red-gold on the horizon.

"What's that?" he asked, pointing.

He turned Storm in the direction of the light. As they drew closer, Tom could see that it was a blazing clump of cacti. Flames roared into the sky, devouring the spiny stems. A short distance away another clump was on fire.

"That's what the nomad said," he reminded Elenna. "The heat from the valley is so great that it sets the cacti alight. We're on the right track!"

The trail of the burning cacti led gently downwards; rocks appeared among the sand dunes. Tom drew his sword, ready at any moment for Kragos and Kildor to leap out of hiding. But nothing moved.

At last the heat began to ebb as the sun went down. An icy wind sprang up, blowing sand into their faces. The flames that burnt the cacti died away, leaving blackened stumps behind.

"Do you think we should stop and sleep?" Elenna asked. "It's freezing now."

Tom could feel her shivering. "I don't think we can," he replied, glancing up to where the moon floated over the sand dunes. "This is our last chance to find the Cup of Life, before King Hugo and Wizard Aduro are turned into half-people."

That wasn't Tom's only reason. Elenna's face was pale and haggard with pain. *If she goes to sleep in these freezing temperatures*, he thought, *she might never wake up.*

CHAPTER FOUR

DUAL DANGER

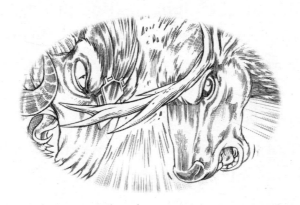

Tom slid to the ground and began to lead Storm, with Elenna slumped in the saddle. They went on following the trail of the burnt-out clumps of cacti, facing straight into the icy wind. Tom raised his shield to protect them from the worst of the blast.

The desert looked eerie in the silver moonlight. Tom struggled to stay alert, in case Kragos and Kildor were lurking nearby. But still there was no sign of the dual Beast.

They stopped briefly to rest in the middle of the night, sharing the last of their provisions and taking a drink of water. Tom shook his water bottle as he fastened it onto Storm's saddle. There were only a few drops left.

"How's your arm?" he asked Elenna, suppressing a yawn.

"Hurting." Elenna seemed barely conscious.

Tom squeezed more of the sagebrush juice onto Elenna's wound and it seemed to revive her a little. Then they went on across a bleak stretch of rocks and sand.

The moon set, leaving them to grope their way across the desert by starlight. At last the freezing wind dropped. Then Tom gradually realised that a pale light was growing on the horizon. Dawn had come – and with it their last chance to find the Cup of Life and complete their Quest.

Now the track led more steeply downwards. Tom could see huge boulders scattered among the dunes ahead of them, outlined against a dull red glow. Waves of fierce heat rolled out to meet Tom and his friends as they approached.

"We must be getting close," Tom said.

Elenna gave a vague murmur of agreement.

Tom let Storm's reins drop and he drew his sword. Raising his shield to protect himself against the heat, he advanced towards the boulders and squeezed through a gap between them.

Tom let out a gasp as he saw what lay beyond the barrier. On the other side of the boulders was a huge pit; flames roared up from it into the sky, though Tom couldn't tell what was feeding them. Nestling at the heart of the fire was the Cup of Life.

Relief swept over Tom as he saw that the cup was still a dull coppery colour. It hadn't been in the fire long enough to glow gold.

Elenna stumbled up to stand beside Tom, leaning against his shoulder. "I tied Storm to a bush back there," she said, gesturing towards a clump of bushes well away from the pit. "And I told Silver to stay with him. I didn't want them getting any closer to the fire."

"Good idea," Tom responded.

"Is it the cup?" Elenna asked, peering over the rim of Tom's shield. "Are we in time?"

"Yes, look," Tom replied. "The cup isn't ready yet, so it doesn't have any magic. Malvel can't have drunk from it. There's still time to put everything right."

Elenna sagged against the nearest boulder, smiling through her pain. "Then all we have to do is get it!"

Tom took a step towards the pit,

but before he could go any further
he heard a tremendous roar coming
from the other side of the fire,
drowning out the noise of the flames.
A huge ram charged from behind
another of the massive boulders. His
fleece was red-gold, thickly curling;
his horns coiled and ended in sharp
points.

"Kildor!" Tom exclaimed.

The Beast let out another bellow and hurtled towards Tom. Elenna unslung her bow and loosed an arrow at the furious creature. It struck Kildor on the shoulder but it didn't halt his charge.

Tom spun round so that his back was to one of the boulders and braced himself for the clash. Kildor's horns struck Tom's shield, jarring his arm and lifting him off his feet as the Beast flung him back against the rock. Tom gasped as the air was driven out of his body.

Summoning every ounce of skill, Tom struck downwards, his sword blade chopping at Kildor's neck. The Beast let out a roar of pain and fury. Blood spattered out of the wound as he reared up on his hind legs and battered at Tom's shield with his forelegs.

For a moment Tom was afraid his shield would give way. Then another arrow struck Kildor in the side and the Beast wheeled away to charge at Elenna, who loosed another arrow before dodging behind one of the boulders.

"Well done!" Tom yelled.

She's a real hero! he thought. *She's badly hurt, but she can still fight.*

Tom raced after Kildor and drove his sword into the ram's side. Kildor stumbled to his knees. As Tom raised his sword for the final stroke, the Beast made a low, rumbling noise in his throat.

A loud bellow answered it, and the ground began to tremble. From behind a nearby sand dune, Kragos galloped into sight. Kildor scrambled up again; Tom's sword-stroke almost

missed him, merely slicing a shallow
cut into his shoulder.

The two giant Beasts faced each
other, stamping their front hooves
into the ground and throwing up
spurts of sand.

"What are they doing?" Elenna asked, appearing at Tom's side. "Are they going to fight each other?"

Kragos and Kildor charged at each other, their heads lowered. Kragos's horns clashed with Kildor's antlers. His wounds vanished as he reared upright to stand on his hind legs. Kragos's body melted into his, so that from the waist up he was a deer.

Tom found he was staring at the dual Beast he had seen outside his uncle's forge. They wore the thick leather belt studded with silver discs, and tiny golden flames licked all over their joined body, surrounding it in a shimmering globe of light.

No, Tom thought. He lowered his sword, briefly stunned by the transformation. *Now they're twice as strong!*

Then he took a deep breath, gripping his sword more tightly. "Come on," he shouted, taking a pace towards the monster. "I'm not afraid of you!"

CHAPTER FIVE

BATTLE AGAINST THE BEAST

Kragos and Kildor slid one of the silver discs out of their belt and hurled it towards Tom, its wickedly sharp edge glistening in the growing daylight. Tom dodged to the side and the disc sliced into a nearby cactus.

Tom laughed scornfully. "Missed!"

Another disc was already spinning through the air. Tom ducked, and at

the same moment, a third disc
thudded into his shield. He crouched
behind it and tried to force his way
forward to attack the Beast, but the
air was filled with the deadly silver
weapons. Summoning all his speed,
he leapt nimbly from side to side, the
silver discs hitting the ground around
his skipping feet. One of them struck

his shoulder, scything through his jerkin and spinning him round. Tom felt a sharp sting and saw the disc still embedded in his arm. He tugged it out and threw it aside as blood welled up from the cut.

"Over here, Beast!" Elenna's voice sounded hoarse with pain.

From the corner of his eye Tom spotted her drawing back her bow again, distracting Kragos and Kildor from following up their attack. She loosed the arrow at the Beast, but her strength was giving way. The shaft buried itself in the ground, far short of its target.

Kragos and Kildor let out a fierce bellow. They swung round and thumped the ground with their hooves as they prepared to attack Elenna.

"No!" Tom yelled. "Cowards! Leave her alone!"

He flung himself between Elenna and the furious Beast. Kragos and Kildor lowered their heads and charged. Tom leapt aside at the last moment and swung his sword with all the strength he could muster, aiming for the Beast's double set of horns.

The sword blade hit the horns with a mighty clang, then bounced harmlessly off them. *No!* Tom gritted his teeth with frustration. Both sets of horns were razor sharp, and far too hard for his sword to bite into. *I can't destroy them – so what am I going to do?*

Tom saw that Elenna had taken shelter again behind one of the boulders. Kragos and Kildor wheeled round, pawing at the ground as they prepared to attack Tom.

He gripped his sword and waited for the onslaught. Then he had an idea. *I can't destroy their horns, but maybe I can use the horns against the Beast.*

Tom remembered Wizard Aduro telling him that the Beast used their dual nature to defeat their enemies. Perhaps there was a way to use that dual nature against the Beast?

This had better work, Tom thought. *If it doesn't, then this Quest – and the whole kingdom of Avantia – are surely doomed.*

Tom judged the distance between himself and the Beast. He heard a startled cry from Elenna, but he had no time to explain his plan to her.

"Trust me!" he called out.

He swiftly ran to meet Kragos and Kildor as they charged towards him, then slipped aside and began to run around them as fast as he could.

Kragos and Kildor let out a roar of anger and frustration. They turned in circles, trying to attack Tom, but he was too quick for them. Soon he could see that both heads were getting dizzy.

As soon as he was sure that the Beast was thoroughly confused, Tom ran straight at them. Using one of Kildor's knees for leverage, he sprang up and tumbled high over their heads, turning over and over in the air.

The two heads reached for Tom as he soared above them. The Beast was trying to gouge Tom's body with their twisted horns and cruel antlers. But Tom was out of their reach. The ram's horns tangled with the stag's antlers. When the Beast tried to tug their two heads apart, they remained locked tightly together.

Yes! Tom landed lightly on the ground and spun round to watch Kragos and Kildor as they struggled to separate themselves. Staggering, the Beast bellowed with fury and terror. Their heads thrashed as they tried to free themselves, but all their efforts only tangled them even more.

Tom looked round for Elenna. He caught sight of her beyond the boulders, kneeling at the edge of the pit of fire. As he watched, she carefully unfastened the water bottle hanging from her belt and tipped the remaining water over her handkerchief. Her movements were slow and shaky; Tom knew she was using up the last of her strength.

As Tom headed towards Elenna she wrapped the soaked material around her hand. Then she thrust her hand into the fire and lifted out the Cup of Life. A golden glow surrounded the cup, fierce and beautiful.

It's ready now, Tom thought. *Its magic has been restored.*

Before he could speak to Elenna, a roar of rage echoed from the sky, drowning out the furious bellows of the Beast.

"Malvel!" Tom cried out with anger. He drew his sword from its scabbard and raised the blade towards the sky. But he could see nothing of the evil wizard, not even his face in the billowing smoke and flame that rose from the pit.

The roar of the defeated wizard went on and on. Tom suddenly saw that Kragos and Kildor had stopped struggling. They stood as still as a statue carved out of stone.

As Tom watched, he saw the interlocked horns begin to crumble. The Beast's heads lost their shape; Kragos and Kildor sank to their knees as their body disintegrated with a final drawn-out moan. Soon they were no more than a heap of sand. A wind sprang up and blew the sand away, scattering it over the face of the desert.

The evil sorcerer's cry of rage died away. Tom ran towards Elenna, but before he reached her she turned towards him, holding up the Cup of Life. She was smiling and her eyes were brilliant.

"Look, Tom!" she exclaimed. "I've got the cup!"

Then she collapsed on the ground, and the cup rolled away from her hand.

Tom flung himself to his knees beside his friend. Elenna was shaking uncontrollably. Her face was white and damp with sweat, and even in the scorching air around the fire her lips were blue. Her breath was fast and shallow.

An evil chuckle sounded in the air; Tom clenched his teeth against a yell of fury. Raging at Malvel wouldn't help his friend.

Horror surged through Tom as he looked into Elenna's face. *She's dying!*

CHAPTER SIX

HOME AGAIN

"No…" Tom whispered.

Gently, he unwrapped the handkerchief from Elenna's hand. The heat of the fire had dried most of the water, but it was still slightly damp. Tom reached for the Cup of Life, which lay on its side. It glowed a brilliant gold, though it didn't burn Tom at all when he picked it up.

Tom squeezed the handkerchief

until a few drops of water trickled
into the cup. Then he raised Elenna's
head and held the cup to her lips.

"Come on, Elenna," he coaxed her.
"You've got to drink this."

Elenna's eyelids fluttered and she
let out a faint moan, but she didn't
try to drink.

"Come on," Tom repeated, fighting back panic. How long would the golden glow last before the magic faded again? "We've finished the Quest. We've found the Cup of Life and we can go home again. But I'm not going anywhere without you."

Elenna opened her eyes. "Tom?" she murmured. "Is that really the Cup of Life?"

"It really is," Tom assured her. "Don't you remember, you pulled it out of the fire? Now you've got to drink from it."

He tilted the cup against Elenna's lips and let the few drops of water trickle into her mouth. With an effort Elenna swallowed. She let out an exhausted sigh, her eyes closed again and she let her head droop against Tom's shoulder.

"Elenna?" Tom said, alarmed.

His friend's violent shaking died away. Gradually her face flushed and the blue colour of her lips faded. Her breathing became slow and deep. She looked as if she were sleeping normally.

Then Elenna's eyes flew open. "Tom, what's going on?" She scrambled to her feet and looked around wildly. "Where's the Beast?"

"The Beast is dead," Tom told her, swallowing a lump in his throat as he saw his friend strong and well again. "It turned to sand when you took the Cup of Life out of the fire."

"*I* took it...?" For a moment Elenna looked puzzled, then her face cleared. "I remember now." She pulled up her sleeve to examine the wound on her arm. But her skin was smooth and firm again; there wasn't even a scar.

Elenna laughed with surprise. "The Cup of Life really works. It's cured me!"

Relief and happiness flooded through Tom. "It really does," he said with a wide grin. "All we have to do now is take it home with us."

He rose to his feet with the Cup of Life in his hand. Already the golden glow was dying and turning the same coppery colour it had been when he first saw it in the fire pit. It would have to be returned to fire before its magic would work again.

With Elenna by his side, Tom walked back to the clump of bushes where they had left Storm and Silver. The grey wolf leapt up as they came into sight and raced to meet Elenna, nosing at her with an anxious whine.

"Don't worry, boy." Elenna stooped

down to plunge her hands into Silver's thick neck fur and draw him into a hug. "I'm fine now."

Storm let out a whinny of welcome as Tom headed for him to stow the Cup of Life away in his saddlebag. For a moment he wondered how they were going to reach the edge of the Ruby Desert with no water and the sun burning down on them.

Then a blue shimmer appeared in the air in front of him. It strengthened into a bright glow and the figure of Wizard Aduro appeared within it. The good wizard looked strong and healthy again. King Hugo stood just behind him, a broad smile on his face.

"Congratulations, Tom and Elenna," Aduro said. "You have saved the Cup of Life, and our lives as well. Thank you."

"The whole of Avantia owes its
gratitude," King Hugo added. "You
have defeated Malvel and made the
kingdom safe for the future."

Elenna had gone pink with
embarrassment. "We only did what
we had to do."

"And we'd do it again," Tom
declared. "We're always ready to take
on new Quests."

"We know your courage well,"

King Hugo replied. "But let's hope that Avantia will be peaceful for a while."

"And now the Cup of Life must return to the fire," Wizard Aduro said. "Tom, hold it up."

The copper glow was fading now, and it looked as if it was made of dull, tarnished silver. Tom held it up. Wizard Aduro raised his hand and blue fire flashed from his fingers. Tom took a step back in astonishment as the Cup of Life vanished.

"It has returned to your uncle's forge," Aduro explained. "Let us hope it will stay there for many years more. And now it's time for you to go back, too," he added.

Wizard Aduro raised his hand again. This time the blue flash was brighter, surrounding Tom and

Elenna and their animal friends in a shimmering blue glow. As it faded, Elenna let out a cry of amazement.

Aduro and King Hugo had vanished. The barren sand dunes of the Ruby Desert had been replaced by the fresh green grass at the edge of Errinel. Tom and his friends stood on the path that led to his uncle and aunt's cottage and the forge.

The sun was shining as Tom led Storm down the path towards the cottage. Elenna walked beside him while Silver sniffed into hollows and under bushes at the side of the path.

As they drew closer to the cottage, Tom heard the sound of voices and laughter coming from somewhere beyond it. He exchanged a mystified glance with Elenna.

"What's going on?" he asked.

The door of the cottage stood open. Tom could see there was no one inside. There was no sound of hammering from the forge, either. Tom led the way back past the cottage and along the street towards the sounds.

Finally the street led into the village square. Tom and Elenna halted at the edge, staring in surprise. A long table stretched across the middle of the square, covered in crisp white cloths and dishes heaped with food. All the villagers were seated on benches.

Tom's father, Taladon, and Uncle Henry were pouring drinks from huge earthenware jugs, while Aunt Maria handed out bread rolls from a large basket.

"It's the party to welcome my father home!" Tom exclaimed.

At the sound of his voice Aunt Maria spun round, dropping her basket, and ran across the square to envelop Tom in a hug.

"You're home safe!" She released Tom to hug Elenna, and added, "You're just in time for the party."

Taladon and Uncle Henry followed Aunt Maria across the square to greet Tom and Elenna, while all the

villagers rose to their feet and started
cheering.

"Did you know we were coming?"
Tom asked, bewildered.

"Yes," Taladon replied, gripping his
son's shoulders. Tom was relieved to
see that his father's burnt hand had
healed. *Thanks to Aunt Maria's herbs*,
he thought.

"Wizard Aduro appeared," Taladon
continued in a low voice. It was
important that most people in

Avantia never knew about Tom's
Quests. "He told me you had finished
your Quest, and that the Cup of Life
is safe in the forge again." His warm
gaze rested on Elenna. "Aduro told
me what a bad time you had, and
how brave you were," he said.
"Thank you."

Elenna smiled. "It was worth it, to
help Avantia."

"Come and sit down," Aunt Maria
urged them.

She ushered them to empty seats at the long table, while one of the villagers led Storm away to be unsaddled and fed. Silver bounded across the square to where the village dogs were chewing happily on a pile of bones.

Tom and Elenna sat down. Tom was filled with pride to think that he and Elenna had saved this happy village and the rest of Avantia from the plots of evil Malvel.

But this isn't the end, he thought. He looked over at Elenna, who was watching him, smiling.

"While there's blood in your veins…?" she asked, teasing. It was clear she'd guessed what he was thinking.

Tom grinned and gave a nod. "We'll always be ready for the next Quest!"

JOIN TOM ON HIS NEXT BEAST QUEST SOON!

Win an exclusive
Beast Quest T-shirt and goody bag!

Tom has battled many fearsome Beasts and we want to know
which one is your favourite! Send us a drawing or painting of
your favourite Beast and tell us in 30 words why you think
it's the best.

Each month we will select **three** winners to receive
a Beast Quest T-shirt and goody bag!

Send your entry on a postcard to
BEAST QUEST COMPETITION
Orchard Books, 338 Euston Road, London NW1 3BH.

Australian readers should email:
childrens.books@hachette.com.au

New Zealand readers should write to:
Beast Quest Competition, 4 Whetu Place, Mairangi Bay,
Auckland NZ, or email: childrensbooks@hachette.co.nz

**Don't forget to include your name and address.
Only one entry per child.**

Good luck!

Win an exclusive
Beast Quest T-shirt and goody bag!

Tom has battled many fearsome Beasts and we want to know
which one is your favourite! Send us a drawing or painting of
your favourite Beast and tell us in 30 words why you think
it's the best.

Each month we will select **three** winners to receive
a Beast Quest T-shirt and goody bag!

Send your entry on a postcard to
BEAST QUEST COMPETITION
Orchard Books, 338 Euston Road, London NW1 3BH.

Australian readers should email:
childrens.books@hachette.com.au

New Zealand readers should write to:
Beast Quest Competition, PO Box 3255, Shortland St,
Auckland 1140, NZ or email: childrensbooks@hachette.co.nz

**Don't forget to include your name and address.
Only one entry per child.**

Good luck!

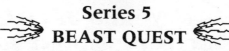

Series 5
BEAST QUEST

Tom must travel to Gwildor, Avantia's twin kingdom,
to free six new Beasts from an evil enchantment...

978 1 40830 437 2   978 1 40830 438 9   978 1 40830 439 6

978 1 40830 440 2   978 1 40830 441 9   978 1 40830 442 6

Can Tom rescue the
precious Cup of Life
from a deadly two-
headed demon?

978 1 40830 436 5